ALSO BY STEPHANIE BARRON

Jane and the Unpleasantness at Scargrave Manor:
Being the First Jane Austen Mystery

Jane and the Man of the Cloth:
Being the Second Jane Austen Mystery

Jane and the Wandering Eye:
Being the Third Jane Austen Mystery

Jane and the Genius of the Place